PRADYUMNA, THE SON OF KRISHNA AND RUKMINI, RODE PROUDLY INTO DWARAKA WITH HIS BRIDE PRABHAVATI, THE DAUGHTER OF THE ASURA, VAJRANABHA, WHOM HE HAD CONQUERED AND SLAIN.

TEARS OF JOY FILLED RUKMINI'S EYES AS SHE LOOKED ON HER SON LEADING PRABHAVATI IN.

THANK GOD YOU ARE SAFE, MY SON! TO COME BACK ALIVE FROM A COMBAT WITH THE INVINCIBLE VAJRANABHA, IS POSSIBLE ONLY WITH DIVINE GRACE.

WHEN THEY REACHED RAIVATAKA, AS THE ELDERS GOT OUT OF THE CHARIOTS AND WALKED TOWARDS THE SACRIFICIAL ENCLOSURE —

COME! THIS IS OUR CHANCE! NO ONE'S LOOKING!

AS SHE RAN BLINDLY INTO THE WOODS, BHANUMATI BUMPED INTO A SAGE.

YOU ILL-MANNERED CHILD!

IT WAS THE IRRITABLE DURVASA, KNOWN FOR HIS BAD TEMPER.

MAY YOU FALL INTO THE HANDS OF YOUR TRADITIONAL FOES.

SAGE NARADA WAS SHOCKED.

O DURVASA, HOW CAN A WISE SOUL LIKE YOU CURSE AN INNOCENT CHILD— AND SO HARSHLY!

LIKE ALL BAD-TEMPERED PEOPLE, DURVASA FELT SORRY FOR HIS RASH WORDS, BUT—

A CURSE ONCE UTTERED BY ME CANNOT BE REVOKED. IT MUST COME TO PASS. HOWEVER . . .

. . . SHE WILL REMAIN UNSULLIED. SHE WILL ALSO MARRY A WORTHY MAN AND BE A HAPPY HOUSEWIFE.

4

AS THE FRIGHTENED GIRLS MADE THEIR WAY BACK TO THE SACRIFICIAL ENCLOSURE —

LET'S NOT BREATHE A WORD OF THIS TO ANYBODY. IT WILL CAUSE THEM UNNECESSARY WORRY...

AND EARN US A SCOLDING!

BESIDES, WHAT THE SAGE SAID CANNOT BE. OUR CITY, GUARDED BY MY FATHER, UNCLES AND GRANDFATHER, IS IMPREGNABLE.

SOON AFTER THE SACRIFICE WAS COMPLETED, KRISHNA AND HIS LARGE FAMILY RETURNED TO DWARAKA, UNAWARE OF THE LITTLE DRAMA IN THE FOREST OF RAIVATAKA.

THE YEARS WENT BY. BHANUMATI GREW UP TO BE A BEAUTIFUL MAIDEN DELIGHTING THE EYES OF ALL AND HER FATHER BHANU * IN PARTICULAR.

I MUST SOON HOLD A SWAYAMVARA FOR HER. THE TESTS FOR THE SUITORS SHALL BE SUCH THAT ONLY THE MOST WORTHY WILL BE ABLE TO WIN HER. I WILL HOLD IT WHEN WE RETURN FROM THE CRUISE.

MEANWHILE AT SHATPURA, VAJRANABHA'S BROTHER, NIKUMBHA, SAT BROODING.

SINCE THAT FATEFUL DAY WHEN I FLED FROM THE BATTLE OF VAJRA AND CAME HERE, I'VE ONLY ONE THOUGHT. I MUST DESTROY THE VAIN YADAVAS.

ALL THESE YEARS OF WAITING HAVE NOT SHOWN ME THE WAY TO AVENGE MY BROTHER'S DEATH.

LORD! LORD! I HAVE GOOD NEWS FOR YOU! DWARAKA IS VIRTUALLY UNGUARDED.

IT WAS ONE OF NIKUMBHA'S SPIES.

AT DWARAKA, BHANUMATI AND HER COMPANIONS WERE OUT IN THE GARDENS OF THE SECLUDED INNER APPARTMENTS OF KRISHNA'S PALACE.

I HEARD THEM TALK ABOUT THE BOAT THEY WERE TO SAIL IN. IT IS MADE OF GOLD AND HAS INNUMERABLE ROOMS. AND EACH ROOM IS ADORNED WITH SAPPHIRES AND PEARLS!

AH! BHANUMATI, IF ONLY WE WERE MARRIED WE TOO COULD HAVE GONE ON THE CRUISE.

I TOO HEARD MY MOTHER AND FATHER TALK ABOUT SOMETHING. IT CONCERNED YOU.

WHAT WERE THEY SAYING?

YOUR FATHER HAS DECIDED TO HOLD A SWAYAMVARA FOR YOU AS SOON AS HE RETURNS, AND...

OH! HAS HE? HE WILL FIRST HAVE TO RESCUE HER FROM MY PALACE AT SHATPURA.

NO! NO!

NIKUMBHA!

WHAT BETTER WAY TO AVENGE MY BROTHER'S DEATH AND DISHONOUR! WHEN THEY COME TO RESCUE HER, I'LL DEFEAT THEM.

HELP! THE ASURA NIKUMBHA!

I'D BETTER MAKE BOTH OF US INVISIBLE.

HELP! HELP! NIKUMBHA IS CARRYING AWAY BHANUMATI.

HEARING THE COMMOTION, UGRASENA AND VASUDEVA RUSHED OUT.

HOW DARE THE VILE FELLOW SET FOOT IN DWARAKA!

WHERE IS HE?

HE HAS VANISHED BEFORE OUR VERY EYES!

KRISHNA TURNED TO ARJUNA.*

COME ON, ARJUNA. HE MUST HAVE HEADED FOR HIS CITY. WE'LL PURSUE HIM ON GARUDA.

PRADYUMNA, YOU FOLLOW US IN YOUR CHARIOT.

KRISHNA THOUGHT OF GARUDA, AND THE GIGANTIC BIRD APPEARED BEFORE HIM.

GARUDA, TAKE US TO SHATPURA.

MEANWHILE —

WE ARE FAR ENOUGH FROM DWARAKA. I CAN SAFELY MAKE OURSELVES VISIBLE NOW.

WHEN BHANUMATI REGAINED CONSCIOUSNESS—

COWARD! DO YOU THINK YOU'LL ESCAPE THE WRATH OF MY UNCLES AND MY GRAND-FATHER?

TAKE ME BACK, AND I'LL ASK THEM TO SPARE YOUR LIFE.

ONCE WE REACH SHAT-PURA, IT IS THEIR LIVES THAT YOU WILL HAVE TO BEG FOR.

WITH SUCH A HEADSTART, I WILL BE SAFE WITHIN MY CITY BEFORE THE YADAVAS REALISE SHE'S MISSING.

AS NIKUMBHA PROCEEDED COMPLACENTLY, A GREAT SHADOW COVERED HIM.

IT'S GARUDA! KRISHNA HAS CAUGHT UP WITH ME!

HE LOOKED BEHIND HIM.

OH! IT'S THE YADAVA WHO STOLE PRABHAVATI'S HEART AND KILLED MY BROTHER.

NIKUMBHA HAD TO THINK FAST.

I'LL USE HER AS A SHIELD AND DEFEND MYSELF.

TERRIFIED, BHANUMATI FAINTED. KRISHNA, ARJUNA AND PRADYUMNA DARED NOT STRIKE NIKUMBHA WITH THEIR MACES.

I'LL USE MY ARROWS. I'LL BE ABLE TO PIERCE HIM WITHOUT HARMING HER.

AND ARJUNA SHOT HIS ARROWS WITH UNERRING PRECISION.

A-A-AH! THE PANDAVA IS NOT KNOWN TO BE THE BEST ARCHER OF ALL TIMES FOR NOTHING. I WILL NOT BE ABLE TO DEFEND MYSELF AND KEEP MY HOLD ON THE GIRL.

SO NIKUMBHA SUDDENLY VANISHED WITH BHANUMATI.

WHERE ARE THEY?

THEY WILL NEVER KNOW WHERE I AM.

BUT NIKUMBHA HAD NOT RECKONED WITH PRADYUMNA.

WAIT, FATHER. MAYAVATI* TAUGHT ME HOW TO EXPOSE THE INVISIBLE.

THERE! THERE HE IS! CHASE HIM.

WHEN THEY WERE CLOSE UPON NIKUMBHA—

I CANNOT MATCH GARUDA'S SPEED. I'LL HAVE TO CHANGE MY FORM.

NIKUMBHA TURNED HIMSELF INTO A YELLOW VULTURE AND . . .

. . . HOLDING BHANUMATI IN HIS TALONS, FLEW ON.

ARJUNA KEPT SHOOTING ARROWS AT HIM, PIERCING HIS VERY VITALS.

BUT NIKUMBHA FLEW ON. SUDDENLY —

I CANNOT FLY ANY FARTHER. ISN'T THAT MOUNT GOKARNA?

TAKING A SUDDEN DIP...

...HE DROPPED DOWN EXHAUSTED.

SEIZING THE OPPORTUNITY, PRADYUMNA CARRIED BHANUMATI INTO HIS CHARIOT.

LEAVE HER AT DWARAKA AND COME BACK. WE'LL FINISH NIKUMBHA.

AS KRISHNA AND ARJUNA ASSAILED HIM, NIKUMBHA LEFT THE NORTHERN RANGE OF GOKARNA...

... AND FLEW TOWARDS SHATPURA.

FASTER, GARUDA! I CAN SEE THE NARROW CAVE—THE ONLY ENTRANCE TO HIS CITY. IF HE ENTERS THE CAVE, HE IS LOST TO US.

GARUDA FLAPPED HIS WINGS AND GAINED SPEED.

BUT WHEN THEY WERE ALMOST UPON HIM, NIKUMBHA ENTERED THE CAVE ...

AH! MY CITY!

...AND WITH HIS LAST OUNCE OF STRENGTH BLOCKED THE INNER ENTRANCE.

ALAS! HE'S GONE. WHAT SHALL WE DO?

WE'LL SPEND THE NIGHT HERE. HE'S BOUND TO COME OUT, THINKING WE'VE GONE AWAY.

EARLY NEXT MORNING, PRADYUMNA RETURNED FROM DWARAKA.

I LEFT HER SAFE WITH BHANU. HE WAS TERRIBLY DEJECTED, AND WONDERED IF HE WOULD EVER FIND A SUITOR FOR HER NOW.

BUT WHERE IS NIKUMBHA?

THE COWARD IS HIDING IN HIS CITY.

I'LL BRING HIM OUT.

PRADYUMNA RAISED HIS VOICE AND BEGAN TO TAUNT NIKUMBHA.

THE ASURAS ARE A VALOROUS PEOPLE INDEED! WHEN ASSAILED, THEY HIDE BEHIND WOMEN OR THE GATES OF THEIR CITY.

THE TAUNT WENT HOME. NIKUMBHA SEETHED WITH FURY.

THE YADAVAS MUST BE TAUGHT A LESSON. I'LL GO OUT AND FINISH THEM.

MAKING HIMSELF INVISIBLE, HE CHARGED OUT OF THE CAVE.

COME, TASTE THE VALOUR OF THE ASURAS.

IMPATIENT TO WREAK VENGEANCE ON THE EVIL ASURA, ARJUNA RAINED ARROWS IN THE DIRECTION OF THE VOICE.

BUT NIKUMBHA RUSHED AT HIM AND STRUCK HIM WITH HIS MACE.

ARJUNA FELL UNCONSCIOUS.

PRADYUMNA USED HIS SUPERNATURAL POWERS TO EXPOSE THE ASURA...

...AND ATTACKED HIM.

BUT HE TOO WAS HIT...

...AND FELL.

BESIDE HIMSELF WITH ANGER, KRISHNA RAISED HIS FINGER.

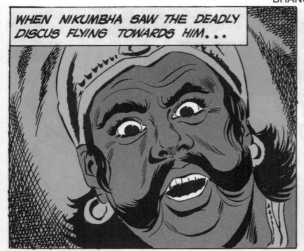

WHEN NIKUMBHA SAW THE DEADLY DISCUS FLYING TOWARDS HIM...

...HE LEFT HIS BODY AND FLED.

HE'S DEAD. THE VERY SIGHT OF MY WEAPON DID IT.

BY THEN, ARJUNA AND PRADYUMNA REGAINED CONSCIOUSNESS.

SUDDENLY —

FATHER! THE WICKED NIKUMBHA IS NOT DEAD. HE HAS ESCAPED LEAVING HIS BODY HERE.

HARDLY HAD PRADYUMNA UTTERED THESE WORDS, WHEN THE BODY OF NIKUMBHA SUDDENLY VANISHED.

ARJUNA AND KRISHNA BURST OUT LAUGHING. THE UNDAUNTED PAIR WERE AMUSED BY THE NEAT TRICK PLAYED ON THEM.

WHILE THEY WERE STILL ROARING WITH LAUGHTER, THEY SUDDENLY SAW THE SKY AND THE EARTH FILLED WITH THOUSANDS OF NIKUMBHAS.

HE HAS SPLIT EACH FRACTION OF HIS BODY INTO SEPARATE BITS AND COVERED EACH BIT WITH AN ILLUSORY BODY. WE'LL DO THE SAME.

AND THE THREE OF THEM TOO SPLIT INTO INNUMERABLE FORMS.

I MUST SEIZE THE FORMS OF ARJUNA. THE DEADLIEST ARROWS ARE HIS.

SO THE VARIOUS FORMS OF NIKUMBHA CAUGHT THE VARIOUS FORMS OF ARJUNA.

AS SOON AS THE INNUMERABLE FORMS OF ARJUNA WERE CAUGHT, THEY FUSED INTO ONE.

THE INNUMERABLE FORMS OF NIKUMBHA TOO FUSED INTO ONE.

I SHALL CARRY HIM AWAY, LEAVE HIM INSIDE MY CITY AND RETURN TO TACKLE THE OTHER TWO.

WHEN KRISHNA AND PRADYUMNA SAW ARJUNA BEING CARRIED AWAY—

LET'S PIERCE HIM WITH OUR ARROWS IN QUICK SUCCESSION AND CUT HIM UP.

BUT TO THEIR AMAZEMENT EACH FRAGMENT OF NIKUMBHA...

... SPRANG UP AS TWO OF HIM; EACH HOLDING AN ARJUNA!

I WILL HAVE TO USE MY DIVINE POWERS AND DISCERN THE TRUE FORM OF NIKUMBHA.

AS SOON AS HE PERCEIVED THE TRUE NIKUMBHA STANDING OUT BRIGHT AND CLEAR FROM THE ILLUSORY ONES...

...KRISHNA TURNED TO PRADYUMNA.

RECEIVE ARJUNA IN YOUR CHARIOT AS HE FALLS.

28

AS PRADYUMNA BROUGHT HIS CHARIOT BENEATH NIKUMBHA, THE DISCUS SEVERED THE HEAD OF THE EVIL ASURA FROM THE BODY...

...AND RETURNED TO KRISHNA.

AS THE ASURA HURTLED DOWN, ARJUNA SLIPPED FROM HIS GRASP.

BUT HE WAS RECEIVED IN PRADYUMNA'S CHARIOT.

AS THE THREE HEROES ENTERED DWARAKA IN TRIUMPH...

... A WAILING BHANU MET THEM.

THE ASURA IS SLAIN. BUT THINK OF THE SHAME! HE ABDUCTED MY DAUGHTER AND TARNISHED HER REPUTATION. WHO WILL MARRY HER NOW?

JUST THEN NARADA APPEARED.

TAKE HEART, BHANU. THERE IS SOMETHING I HAVE TO TELL YOU.

AND NARADA TOLD THEM ABOUT DURVASA'S CURSE AND HIS BLESSINGS.

SO, DO NOT LAMENT. WHAT HAD TO HAPPEN, HAPPENED. GIVE YOUR DAUGHTER TO SAHADEVA, FOR THAT PANDAVA IS VIRTUOUS, HEROIC AND HANDSOME.

PRADYUMNA, SEND AN EMISSARY TO BRING SAHADEVA HERE.

AS SOON AS SAHADEVA REACHED DWARAKA, BHANUMATI WAS MARRIED TO HIM.

AFTER THE WEDDING, AS THE COUPLE LEFT FOR SAHADEVA'S CITY—

THE SAGE'S CURSE DID COME TRUE AFTER ALL. BUT SO HAVE HIS BLESSINGS. WHO WOULD BE A BETTER HUSBAND THAN THIS POWERFUL PANDAVA?

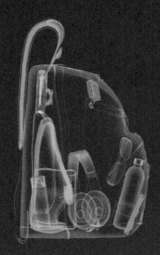